Words for Dr. Y.

ANNE SEXTON

Words for Dr. Y.

Uncollected Poems
with Three Stories

Edited by Linda Gray Sexton

Houghton Mifflin Company Boston

1978

"Dr. Y./I need a thin hot wire" and "Yellow" from this book
appear in the August 1978 issue of *Mademoiselle*.

Library of Congress Cataloging in Publication Data

Sexton, Anne.
   Words for Dr. Y.

   I. Sexton, Linda Gray, date   II. Title.
PS3537.E915W6   811'.5'4   78-7543
ISBN 0-395-27081-2
ISBN 0-395-27268-8 pbk.

Printed in the United States of America

V 10 9 8 7 6 5 4 3 2 1

EDITOR'S NOTE

Words for Dr. Y. is the first collection of Anne Sexton's poetry from which her editorial guidance was totally absent. *45 Mercy Street,* her first posthumous publication, was the last book she actively planned. In preparing *Anne Sexton: A Self-Portrait in Letters,* however, I realized that among her files and manuscripts in progress was a considerable body of valuable material that deserved to be published.

The first section of this book, "Letters to Dr. Y.," written from 1960 to 1970, was originally a series of poems Anne wanted to include in her sixth volume, *The Book of Folly.* When friends and editors convinced her it did not belong there, she specifically reserved it for publication after her death. As far as I know, this is the only time she ever set work aside for such a purpose.*

The second section is composed of poems written between July 1971 and July 1973; she had no chance to incorporate these into a book or to place them with magazines.

Though she had put the series "Scorpio, Bad Spider, Die" in one of her file cabinets beside *45 Mercy Street* and other poems intended for publication, I believe she was actually quite uncertain about its final destination. Although written in the later years of her career, these poems often return to the stricter form, rhyme, and meter of her earlier work. Perhaps this return, coupled with the very personal content of

---

* Originally Anne had intended *The Death Notebooks* for posthumous publication. However, she had a change of heart and the collection appeared in February 1973.

these poems, made her initially uneasy about publishing them, particularly after the mythmaking and free stylistics she had used so successfully in *Transformations* (1971). Also, since the "Scorpio" poems never fit thematically into any book she worked on thereafter, she simply may have been waiting for an appropriate collection in which to include them.

The last section of *Words for Dr. Y.* consists of three horror tales. Anne enjoyed writing these stories perhaps more than anything else she ever produced and was proud of the result. In June of 1974 she asked her agents to send them to magazines. Although their first brief attempts to place them failed, she was determined to find the stories a permanent home.

Anne Sexton wrote many of the poems collected here at a time when her process of revision was still quite rigorous, and therefore this volume may seem more finished than *45 Mercy Street*. Still, it must be remembered that she honed her manuscripts right up until the last minute; as with *45 Mercy Street*, much that is included here might well have been rewritten had she been alive to edit the poems herself. In choosing what to publish, I could only try to approximate her hand.

Editing this collection involved only a process of selection; as in *45 Mercy Street*, everything in *Words for Dr. Y.* appears as originally written. However, I have deleted a few poems from Parts I and III that I felt would not add to the reader's understanding of Anne's poetry or life.

Anne Sexton's final poems were written between March and October of 1974. These last will be included in a forthcoming volume of her collected work.

Linda Gray Sexton
December 4, 1977

CONTENTS

Letters to Dr. Y.

(1960-1970)

Dr. Y.
I need a thin hot wire,
your Rescue Inc. voice
to stretch me out,
to keep me from going underfoot
and growing stiff
as a yardstick.

Death,
I need your hot breath,
my index finger in the flame,
two cretins standing at my ears,
listening for the cop car.

Death,
I need a little cradle
to carry me out,
a boxcar for my books,
a nickel in my palm,
and no kiss
on my kiss.

Death,
I need my little addiction to you.
I need that tiny voice who,
even as I rise from the sea,

all woman, all there,
says kill me, kill me.
My manic eye
sees only the trapeze artist
who flies without a net.
Bravo, I cry,
swallowing the pills,
the do die pills.
Listen ducky,
death is as close to pleasure
as a toothpick.
To die whole,
riddled with nothing
but desire for it,
is like breakfast
after love.

February 16, 1960

I have words for you, Dr. Y.,
words for sale.
Words that have been hoarded up,
waiting for the pleasure act of coming out,
hugger-mugger, higgily-piggily
onto the stage.

And where is the order? you will ask.

A disorderly display of words,
one after the other.
It's a huge gathering ball of words,
not a snowball, but an old string ball,
one from the rag bag.

And where is the order? you will ask.

Words out through the lips like toads!
And if there is a pearl among them
she will surely get lost in the confusion.
Words, words, words,
piled up one on another,
making a kind of weight of themselves.
    1. each less than a pound
    2. each less than a stick of butter
    3. one the size of a roasted peanut, light and wrinkled

4. another one, a slim precise girl, a sunflower seed
5. one, as small as my thumb, a beach stone in the hand
6. and there is always that one, the toad. The toad
has many brothers.

And where is the order? you will ask.

Words waiting, angry, masculine,
with their fists in a knot.
Words right now, alive in the head,
heavy and pressing as in a crowd.
Pushing for headroom, elbowing,
knowing their rights.

And where is the order? you will ask.

A word, a sunflower seed.
One we would surely overlook.
So easily lost, a dead bee.
So vulnerable.
She is already trampled, that one,
having traveled so far from the heart.
She weighs so little.
She is so light and vulnerable.
She is the dead bee called love.

June 6, 1960

My three poets!
John, Maxine, George.
We meet once a month
like the moon,
like the menses.

We weep together
and make a bed for rain.

None of them has
the sense of evil that I have,
evil that jaw breaker,
that word-wife.

January 1, 1961

I begin again, Dr. Y.,
this neverland journal,
full of my own sense of filth.
Why else keep a journal, if not
to examine your own filth?

January 1, 1962

I love the word warm.
It is almost unbearable —
so moist and breathlike.
I feel the earth like a nurse,
curing me of winter.
I feel the earth,
its worms oiling upward,
the ants ticking,
the oak leaf rotting like feces
and the oats rising like angels.

In the beginning,
summer is a sense
of this earth,
or of yourself.

June 3, 1962

This loneliness is just an exile from God.

April 1, 1963

I remember my mother dying . . .
a strange feeling to know that life is just
going out of you with every breath.
Strange walls and colors.
The nurses coming and going.
White, white, mother I am leaving.
Faces, suddenly suspended above you;
faces that you think it's your business to love
if only you could remember their names.
Pain and never knowing that you are getting ugly.
The fog of medication and old ether dreams.
White. White.
Perhaps the ugliness is that of a new baby —
growing back to your first skull.

And all this with a memory of attics
and dining room wallpaper, the A & P
and the superhighway and those small roads —
roadways where you've never been
and that you would like to speak of if
you could remember how to form the words.
White, white, mother I am leaving.

A baby just lies there
having come from its bath;
lies there getting used to being outside the bath,

lies there getting used to being outside of something,
while you, death-child, lie fitfully
waiting to go inside.

And surely the people clasp at your bedsheet
and your railing and peer at you through
your tubes and rustle the bedside flowers.
White, white.

Oh there is no use in loving the dying.
I have tried.
I have tried but you can't,
you just can't guard the dead.
You are the watchman and you
can't keep the gate shut.

March 14, 1964

I put some daisies in a bowl
with a weed that looks like babies'-breath.
I put them in that bowl to show
my husband I am here. I care.
They are steady in their sleep.
Daisies in water are the longest lasting
flower you can give to someone.
Fact.
Buy daisies.
Not roses.
Yes daisies.
Buy them for everyone, sick or well.
Buy them for well people especially.

Name your girl-child Daisy
or name your heroine Daisy
and watch her sun-heart with its inner urges
and her chalk petals stick straight up
like doll's thumbs.
But let her bend her head sadly
now and then for sometimes her palm
will read *He loves me not.*

But not always.

June 14, 1964

What has it come to, Dr. Y.
my needing you?
I work days,
stuffed into a pine-paneled box.
You work days
with your air conditioner gasping
like a tube-fed woman.
I move my thin legs into your office
and we work over the cadaver of my soul.
We make a stage set out of my past
and stuff painted puppets into it.
We make a bridge toward my future
and I cry to you: I will be steel!
I will build a steel bridge over my need!
I will build a bomb shelter over my heart!
But my future is a secret.
It is as shy as a mole.

What has it come to
my needing you . . .
I am the irritating pearl
and you are the necessary shell.
You are the twelve faces of the Atlantic
and I am the rowboat. I am the burden.

How dependent, the fox asks?
Why so needy, the snake sings?

It's this way . . .
Time after time I fall down into the well
and you dig a tunnel in the dangerous sand,
you take the altar from a church and shore it up.
With your own white hands you dig me out.
You give me hoses so I can breathe.
You make me a skull to hold the worms
of my brains. You give me hot chocolate
although I am known to have no belly.
The trees are whores yet you place
me under them. The sun is poison
yet you toss me under it like a rose.
I am out of practice at living.
You are as brave as a motorcycle.

What has it come to
that I should defy you?
I would be a copper wire
without electricity.
I would be a Beacon Hill dowager
without her hat.
I would be a surgeon
who cut with his own nails.
I would be a glutton
who threw away his spoon.
I would be God
without Jesus to speak for me.

I would be Jesus
without a cross to prove me.

August 24, 1964

15

Blue eyes wash off sometimes.
They have already torn up the sky
for they have torn off its color.
Also they have swallowed up the salt
and this, in turn, closes up the beaches.

Mr. God,
why are you that blue?

Blue eyes I'm married to.

But brown eyes where Father Inc. waits,
that little Freud shoveling dirt in the cellar,
that Mr. Man, Mr. Cellar Man, brown as
old blood.

February 23, 1965

I called him *Comfort*.
Dr. Y., I gave him the wrong name.
I should have called him *Preacher*
for all day there on the coastland
he read me the Bible.
He read me the Bible to prove I was sinful.
For in the night he was betrayed.
And then he let me give him a Judas-kiss,
that red lock that held us in place,
and then I gave him a drink from my cup
and he whispered, "Rape, rape."
And then I gave him my wrist
and he sucked on the blood,
hating himself for it,
murmuring, "God will see. God will see."

And I said,
"To hell with God!"

And he said,
"Would you mock God?"

And I said,
"God is only mocked by believers!"

And he said,
"I love only the truth."

And I said,
"This holy concern for the truth —
no one worries about it except liars."

And God was bored.
He turned on his side
like an opium eater
and slept.

March 28, 1965

Dr. Y., I have a complaint.
Why do you smile that liverish smile?
Why do you double over in a spaz and a swoon,
gurgling on my past, my grief, my bile?
Am I a joke?
Am I a gas?

Everything I say to you is awfully serious.
I don't make puns.
I have no slips of tongue.
I pay in cold hard cash.
I am prompt as you have noted.
I am among the few who make songs.
My sisters laughed at me always.
When I drew pictures they laughed.
When I danced they laughed.
When I wrote they laughed.
When I ate they laughed.

Ha-ha-ha.

Urine and tears pour out of me.
I'm the one you broke.

February 14, 1966

What do the voices say? Dr. Y. asks.

My voices are as real as books, I answer.

They say,
"We are your voices. When you look at your soup
one of us is here saying, '*You!* You're on trial
and if you tell, then Nana will choke you
and no sane man will believe you and your face
will grow as black as a German stump.' "

Voice number one says,
"I am the leaves. I am the martyred.
Come unto me with death for I am the siren.
I am forty young girls in green shells.
Come out of your house and come unto me
for I am silk and convalescent."

Voice number two says,
"Choke on me. I am the rock in front
of your window. I am a pit to gag on.
I am male and I will take my sword blade
and cut loose your children and your mate.
I am a large puppet. I am Mr. Gobblegook."

Voice number three says,
"I am the white clown. I am whitewashed.
I am nothing but salt and powder
and I spit on you for you are impure.
Your Nana had white powdery hair, eh?
My whisper goes crazy even in you."

Voice number four says,
"I am the razor. I am so humble
in your little white medicine chest.
I am alert. My language is a thin whine.
Have you ever thought, my single one,
that your hands are thorns to be cut to the quick?"

Voice number five says,
"I am a whip. Could you not find
someone to put me to a proper use?
I will cut. I will make blood into brine.
I will mark you all over with little red fish.
You will be almost killed, a delight.
You will suffer, child, and it will be kind."

June 6, 1967

It's music you've never heard
that I've heard,
that makes me think of you —
not Villa Lobos, my heart's media,
but pop songs on my kitchen radio
bleating like a goat.
I know a little bit
about a lot of things
but I don't know enough about you . . .
Songs like cherries in a bowl,
sweet and sour and small.
Suddenly I'm not half the girl
I used to be.
There's a shadow hanging over me . . .
From me to you out of my electric devil
but easy like the long skirts
in a Renoir picnic with clouds and parasols.

Fourteen boys in cars are parked
with fourteen girls in cars and they
are listening to our song with one blood.
No one is ruined. Everyone is in
a delight at this ardor.

I am in a delight with you, Music Man.
Your name is Dr. Y. My name is Anne.

November 18, 1967

I am no longer at war with sin,
working daily with my little shield and paddle
against those willful acts,
those small loaves,
those drops of angel sperm.

And yet and yet . . .
the old sense of evil remains,
evil that wife.
Evil who leaves me here,
most days,
dead broke.

She is a commercial woman.
She waits at the gate.
She dogs me on the street.
She shuts me in a lavatory.
She is my other face,
grunting as I sigh,
vomiting as I chew.

Take adultery or theft.
Merely sins.
It is evil who dines on the soul,
stretching out its long bone tongue.
It is evil who tweezers my heart,
picking out its atomic worms.

December 4, 1967

Remember *The Shadow Knows?*
And he did. He could see me
squatting there beside my sensible brown radio.
And it goes on. It goes on even now.
They all see you when you least suspect.
Out flat in your p.j.'s glowering at T.V.
or at the oven gassing the cat
or at the Hotel 69 head to knee.

Didn't you know it, Dr. Y.,
you're news to someone? Someone's
got a secret file in case you resist,
in case you light a fuse. Take,
for instance, the druggist.
Have you seen him eyeball and smile,
meanwhile keeping tabs on what you're taking?
He's the FBI of sleeping and the FBI of waking.

April Fools' Day 1968

What about all the psychotics
of the world?
Why do they keep eating?
Why do they keep making plans
and meeting people at the appointed time?
Don't they know there is nothing,
a void, an eyeless socket,
a grave with the corpse stolen?
Don't they know that God gave them
their miraculous sickness
like a shield, like armor
and if their eyes are in the wrong
part of their heads, they shouldn't complain?
What are they doing seeing their doctors
when the world's up for grabs.

January 12, 1969

As Ruth said, "Enlarge the place of thy tent."

July 4, 1969

I'm dreaming the My Lai soldier again,
I'm dreaming the My Lai soldier night after night.
He rings the doorbell like the Fuller Brush Man
and wants to shake hands with me
and I do because it would be rude to say no
and I look at my hand and it is green
with intestines.
And they won't come off,
they won't. He apologizes for this over and over.
The My Lai soldier lifts me up again and again
and lowers me down with the other dead women and babies
saying, *It's my job. It's my job.*

Then he gives me a bullet to swallow
like a sleeping tablet.
I am lying in this belly of dead babies
each one belching up the yellow gasses of death
and their mothers tumble, eyeballs, knees, upon me,
each for the last time, each authentically dead.
The soldier stands on a stepladder above us
pointing his red penis right at me and saying,
Don't take this personally.

December 17, 1969

What are the leaves saying? you ask.

I am not allowed to repeat it.
There are rules about this.

What is it like? you ask.

Words for it crawl in and out of me
like worms. I do not like them.
And yet my heart thumps like applause.

There are warnings . . .

What are the leaves saying? you ask.

Orders. Demands.

What do the leaves remind you of? you ask.

Green. Green!

What does green remind you of? you ask.

Weed memories.
A fisherman with green fruit in his net . . .
The back lawn I danced on when I was eight . . .

The slime pool that the dog drowned in . . .
A drunk vomiting up a teaspoon of bile . . .
Washing the polio off the grapes when I was ten . . .
A Harvard book bag in Rome . . .
Night baseball games . . .
Lake Como . . .
But those are painted colors.
Only the leaves are human.

Human? you ask.

They are girls. Green girls.
Death and life is their daily work.
Death seams up and down the leaf.
I call the leaves my death girls.
The death girls turn at the raggedy edge
and swim another length down the veins
to the raggedy heart.

And these death girls sing to you? you ask.

Yes.

And does it excite you? you ask.

Yes.
It's a canker-suicide high.
It's a sisterhood.
I need to be laid out at last
under them, as straight as a pea pod.
To die whole. To die as soft and young as a leaf.
To lie down whole in that green god's belly.

Have the leaves always talked? Even when you were young?
   you ask.

When I was five.I played under pines.
Pines that were stiff and sturdy.
State of Maine pines sifting the air
like harps, sifting over that fifth me.
Dark green.
A different order.
A different sign.
I was safe there at five under that stiff crotch.

The leaves tell you to die? you ask.

Yes.

A strange theater.

                                        May 5, 1970

afe, safe psychosis is broken.
ıs hard.
ıs made of stone.
vered my face like a mask.
ıt has cracked.
ıy I drove a train through it looking for my mouth.
 then I fed it.
ı Dr. Y.'s hands I fed it.

ittle illustrated armor,
ıard, hard shell has cracked
)r. Y. held my hand
vith that touch
ead father rode on the Superchief
 to me with dollar bills in his fist
ny dead mother started to knit me a sweater
old me, as usual, to sit up straight,
ny dead sister danced into the room
rrow something and I said
es, yes.

ıand in his hand,
ıily of fingers,
o leaf.
d I have attended thee.
h I have attended thee.

But now touch is here.
Touch is difficult.
Touch is the revolution.
Now tears run down me like Campbell's Soup.
Now the Lord hath given me my petition.

Your hand is the outrageous redeemer.

July 21, 1970

I begin to see. Today I am not all wood.

September 3, 1970

I am happy today with the sheets of life.
I washed out the bedsheets.
I hung out the bedsheets and watched them
slap and lift like gulls.
When they were dry I unfastened them
and buried my head in them.
All the oxygen of the world was in them.
All the feet of the babies of the world were in them.
All the crotches of the angels of the world were in them.
All the morning kisses of Philadelphia were in them.
All the hopscotch games on the sidewalks were in them.
All the ponies made of cloth were in them.

So this is happiness,
that journeyman.

November 9, 1970

Poems 1971-1973

BUYING THE WHORE

You are a roast beef I have purchased
and I stuff you with my very own onion.

You are a boat I have rented by the hour
and I steer you with my rage until you run aground.

You are a glass that I have paid to shatter
and I swallow the pieces down with my spit.

You are the grate I warm my trembling hands on,
searing the flesh until it's nice and juicy.

You stink like my Mama under your bra
and I vomit into your hand like a jackpot
its cold hard quarters.

July 15, 1971

TO LIKE, TO LOVE

Aphrodite,
my Cape Town lady,
my mother, my daughter,
I of your same sex
goggling on your right side
have little to say about LIKE and LOVE.
I dream you Nordic and six foot tall,
I dream you masked and blood-mouthed,
yet here you are with kittens and puppies,
subscribing to five ecological magazines,
sifting all the blacks out of South Africa
onto a Free-Ship, kissing them all like candy,
liking them all, but love? Who knows?

I ask you to inspect my heart
and name its pictures.
I push open the door to your heart
and I see all your children sitting around a campfire.
They sit like fruit waiting to be picked.
I am one of them. The one sipping whiskey.
You nod to me as you pass by and I look up
at your great blond head and smile.
We are all singing as in a holiday
and then you start to cry,
you fall down into a huddle,
you are sick.

What do we do?
Do we kiss you to make it better?
No. No. We all walk softly away.
We would stay and be the nurse but
there are too many of us and we are too worried to help.
It is love that walks away
and yet we have terrible mouths
and soft milk hands.
We worry with *like*.
We walk away like *love*.

Daughter of us all,
Aphrodite,
we would stay and telegraph God,
we would mother like six kitchens,
we would give lessons to the doctors
but we leave, hands empty,
because you are no one.

Not ours.
You are someone soft who plays
the piano on Mondays and Fridays
and examines our murders for flaws.

Blond lady,
do you love us, love us, love us?
As I love America, you might mutter,
before you fall asleep.

May 17, 1972

THE SURGEON

for Jack McGinty

Jack, oh big Jack,
of the rack and the screw,
why in New York did you seem
tinier. Doctor Jack,
in your office, in the O.R.
last week unscrewing my hip,
you seemed as big as an island.
I stir my martinis with the screw,
four-inch and stainless steel,
and think of my hip where it lay
for four years like a darkness.
Jack, oh big Jack,
would you like an ear or a finger
to keep of me? From you I have
one of the tools of your carpentry.
But what do you keep of me?
The memory of my bones flying
up into your hands.

June 5, 1972

SPEAKING BITTERNESS

Born like a dwarf
in eighteen ninety-four, the last
of nine children, stuffed in my pram
in Louisburg Square or shortest
to line up at Boothbay Harbor's wharf
where the cunners sulked and no one ever swam.
Blurting through the lobsters and the kelp
we were off to Squirrel Island with five in help.

The cook would vomit
over the rail and the Scotties would bark
and the wind would whip out Old Glory
until the Stewarts, the lots of them, would disembark.
I loved that island like Jesus loves the Jesuit
even though I drowned past Cuckolds' light, another story.
When I was eight Infantile struck. I was the crippled one.
The whole world down the spout, except my skeleton.

They bought a nurse
to live my whole life through
but I've outlived all seventeen
with never a man to say *I do, I do.*
Mother, to be well-born is another curse.
Now I am just an elderly lady who is full of spleen,
who humps around greater Boston in a God-awful hat,
who never lived and yet outlived her time,
hating men and dogs and Democrats.

When I was thirty-two
the doctor kissed my withered limbs
and said he'd leave his wife and run
away with me. Oh, I remember the likes of him,
his hand over my boots, up my skirts like a corkscrew.
The next month he moved his practice to Washington.
Not one man is forgiven! East, West, North, South!
I bite off their dingbats. Christ rots in my mouth.
I curse the seed of my father that put me here
for when I die there'll be no one to say: *Oh No!*
Oh dear.

August 29, 1972

TELEPHONE

Take a red book called TELEPHONE,
size eight by four. There it sits.
My red book, name, address and number.
These are all people that I somehow own.
Yet some of these names are counterfeit.
There beside *Frigidaire* and *Dictaphone*,
there beside Max and Fred and Peggy and John,
beside Eric of Seattle and Snook of Saskatchewan
are all the dear dead names. The ink lies.
Hello! Hello! Goodbye. And then excise.

And thus I do a death dance, a dance
of the thumb. I lay a snake skin
over the name but it won't erase.
I ink my thumbprint. I drool in a trance
and take spit and blood and wine and aspirin
to make a sauce and wipe it on my face.
Then I bite the page, a strange lover of the dead
and my watch dial sings Hello and the name is fed.
Name, I will drown in you like the mother in vinegar
for I have inherited you, a raincheck, a transfer.

And you, witchman, who died without my approval,
you who never loved me although I offered up
every sugar at star-fall, you who blackened
my garden and my hipbone with your chronicle

of my flaws, you who put gum in my coffee cup
and worms in my Jell-O, you who let me pretend
you were daddy of the poets, witchman, you stand
for all, for all the bad dead, a Salvation Army Band
who plays for no one. I am cement. The bird in me is blind
as I knife out your name and all your dead kind.

                              September 11, 1972

YELLOW

When they turn the sun
on again I'll plant children
under it, I'll light up my soul
with a match and let it sing, I'll
take my mother and soap her up, I'll
take my bones and polish them, I'll
vacuum up my stale hair, I'll
pay all my neighbors' bad debts, I'll
write a poem called *Yellow* and put
my lips down to drink it up, I'll
feed myself spoonfuls of heat and
everyone will be home playing with
their wings and the planet will
shudder with all those smiles and
there will be no poison anywhere, no plague
in the sky and there will be a mother-broth
for all of the people and we will
never die, not one of us, we'll go on
won't we?

September 23, 1972

THE DEATH KING

I hired a carpenter
to build my coffin
and last night I lay in it,
braced by a pillow,
sniffing the wood,
letting the old king
breathe on me,
thinking of my poor murdered body,
murdered by time,
waiting to turn stiff as a field marshal,
letting the silence dishonor me,
remembering that I'll never cough again.

Death will be the end of fear
and the fear of dying,
fear like a dog stuffed in my mouth,
fear like dung stuffed up my nose,
fear where water turns into steel,
fear as my breast flies into the Disposall,
fear as flies tremble in my ear,
fear as the sun ignites in my lap,
fear as night can't be shut off,
and the dawn, my habitual dawn,
is locked up forever.

Fear and a coffin to lie in
like a dead potato.

Even then I will dance in my fire clothes,
a crematory flight,
blinding my hair and my fingers,
wounding God with his blue face,
his tyranny, his absolute kingdom,
with my aphrodisiac.

September 1972

THE ERRAND

I've been going right on, page by page,
since we last kissed, two long dolls in a cage,
two hunger-mongers throwing a myth in and out,
double-crossing our lives with doubt,
leaving us separate now, foggy with rage.

But then I've told my readers what I think
and scrubbed out the remainder with my shrink,
have placed my bones in a jar as if possessed,
have pasted a black wing over my left breast,
have washed the white out of the moon at my sink,

have eaten The Cross, have digested its lore,
indeed, have loved that eggless man once more,
have placed my own head in the kettle because
in the end death won't settle for my hypochondrias,
because this errand we're on goes to one store.

That shopkeeper may put up barricades,
and he may advertise cognac and razor blades,
he may let you dally at Nice or the Tuileries,
he may let the state of our bowels have ascendancy,
he may let such as we flaunt our escapades,

swallow down our portion of whiskey and dex,
salvage the day with some soup or some sex,

juggle our teabags as we inch down the hall,
let the blood out of our fires with phenobarbital,
lick the headlines for Starkweathers and Specks,

let us be folk of the literary set,
let us deceive with words the critics regret,
let us dog down the streets for each invitation,
typing out our lives like a Singer sewing sublimation,
letting our delicate bottoms settle and yet

they were spanked alive by some doctor of folly,
given a horn or a dish to get by with, by golly,
exploding with blood in this errand called life,
dumb with snow and elbows, rubber man, a mother wife,
tongues to waggle out the words, mistletoe and holly,

tables to place our stones on, decades of disguises,
until the shopkeeper plants his boot in our eyes,
and unties our bone and is finished with the case,
and turns to the next customer, forgetting our face
or how we knelt at the yellow bulb with sighs
like moth wings for a short while in a small place.

December 2, 1972

THE TWELVE-THOUSAND-DAY
HONEYMOON

The twelve-thousand-day honeymoon
is over.
Hands crumble like clay,
the mouth, its bewildered tongue,
turns yellow with pain,
the breasts with their doll teacups
lie in a grave of silence,
the arms fall down like boards,
the stomach,
so lightly danced over,
lies grumbling in its foul nausea,
the mound that lifted like the waves
again and again
at your touch
stops, lies helpless as a pinecone,
the vagina, where a daisy rooted,
where a river of sperm rushed home,
lies like a clumsy, unused puppet,
and the heart
slips backward,
remembering, remembering,
where the god had been
as he beat his furious wings.
And then the heart
grabs a prayer out of the newspaper
and lets it buzz through its ventricle, its auricle,

like a wasp
stinging where it will,
yet glowing furiously
in the little highways
where you remain.

July 20, 1973

Scorpio, Bad Spider, Die

The Horoscope Poems

(1971)

"And reading my own life with loathing,
I tremble and curse."

— PUSHKIN

MADAME ARRIVES IN THE MAIL

Dear Friend,
*   It may seem to you superstitious and childish to*
consult the Forecast in your daily activities, but the
main object of reading your horoscope should be
self-training and knowledge of yourself and your
character traits.

Madame, I have a confusion,
will you take it away?
Madame, I have a sickness,
will you take it away?
Madame, I am the victim of an odor,
will you take it away?
Take! For God's sake take!
Mend everything!
The moon is always up there pulling and pulling.
Why not let you bring off some occult tricks?
I'd like to nail the moon up there, a sad crucifix,
and inspect its hair, its roots, its glands
and see if the agony dropped from me like sand.
Yes, indeed,
Madame,
you are a soft shape.
You hiss as you go.
I hear the death of me, the murderous weeds,

the stallion breathing sulphur, the hara-kiri rape,
the bludgeon, the bludgeon and the lowering below
into the deep thorax, the big legs of the ground
so I'll give you a year of me, a kind of iron cast
to assess. Take this Scorpio, this death-bitch me
and advise, advise. Madame, bring on your forecast
for I was only sitting here in my white study
with the awful black words pushing me around.

August 18–25, 1971

JANUARY 1st

Today is favorable for joint financial affairs but do not take any chances with speculation.

My daddy played the market.
My mother cut her coupons.
The children ran in circles.
The maid announced, the soup's on.

The guns were cleaned on Sunday.
The family went out to shoot.
We sat in the blind for hours.
The ducks fell down like fruit.

The big fat war was going on.
So profitable for daddy.
She drove a pea green Ford.
He drove a pearl gray Caddy.

In the end they used it up.
All that pale green dough.
The rest I spent on doctors
who took it like gigolos.

My financial affairs are small.
Indeed they seem to shrink.

My heart is on a budget.
It keeps me on the brink.

I tell it stories now and then
and feed it images like honey.
I will not speculate today
with poems that think they're money.

August 26, 1971

JANUARY 19th

*Your home can be helpful to your health through rest
and the care you get from family members.*

Home is my Bethlehem,
my succoring shelter,
my mental hospital,
my wife, my dam,
my husband, my sir,
my womb, my skull.
Never leave it.
Never leave it.

Home is my daughters
pouring cups of tea,
the dumb brown eyes
of my animals, a liqueur
on the rocks, each a guarantee
of the game and the prize.
Never leave it.
Never leave it.

I leave you, home,
when I'm ripped from the doorstep
by commerce or fate. Then I submit
to the awful subway of the world, the awful shop

of trousers and skirts. Oh animal bosom,
let me stay! Let me never quit
the sweet cereal, the sweet thumb!

August 27–September 8, 1971

JANUARY 24th

Originality is important.

I am alone here in my own mind.
There is no map
and there is no road.
It is one of a kind
just as yours is.
It's in a vapor. It's in a flap.
It makes jelly. It chews toads.
It's a dummy. It's a whiz.
Sometimes I have to hunt her down.
Sometimes I have to track her.
Sometimes I hold her still and use a nutcracker.

Such conceit! Such maggoty thoughts,
such an enormous con
just cracks me up.
My brown study will do me in
gushing out of me cold or hot.
Yet I'd risk my life
on that dilly dally buttercup
called dreams. She of the origin,
she of the primal crack, she of the boiling
beginning, she of the riddle, she keeps me here,
toiling and toiling.

[undated]

63

FEBRUARY 3rd

Your own ideas may be too fanciful to be practical.

My ideas are a curse.
They spring from a radical discontent
with the awful order of things.
I play clown. I play carpenter. I play nurse.
I play witch. Each like an advertisement
for change. My husband always plays King
and is continually shopping in his head for a queen
when only clown, carpenter, nurse, witch can be seen.

Take my LIBRARY CAPER.
I took thirty experts from our town
and each bought thirty expert books.
On an October night when witchery can occur
we each stole thirty books, we took them down
from the town library shelves, each of us a crook,
and placed them in the town dump, all that lovely paper.
We left our expert books upon the shelves. My library caper.

One night we crashed a wedding dinner,
but not the guests. We crashed the chef.
We put dollar bills in the salad, right beside
the lettuce and tomatoes. Our salad was a winner.
The guests kept picking out the bucks, such tiny thefts,
and cawing and laughing like seagulls at their landslide.

There was a strange power to it. Power in that lovely paper.
The bride and groom were proud. I call it my Buck Wedding
    Caper.

My own ideas are a curse for a king and a queen.
I'm a wound without blood, a car without gasoline
unless I can shake myself free of my dog, my flag,
of my desk, my mind, I find life a bit of a drag.
Not always, mind you. Usually I'm like my frying pan —
useful, graceful, sturdy and with no caper, no plan.

August 28, 1971

FEBRUARY 4th

The day is good for attempts to advance a secret hope
or dream.

It's a room I dream about.
I had it twice. Two years out of forty-two.
Once at nine. Once more at thirty-six.
There I was dragging the ocean, that knock-out,
in and out by its bottle-green neck, letting it chew
the rocks, letting it haul beach glass and furniture sticks
in and out. From my room I controlled the woman-of-war,
that Mary who came in and in opening and closing the door.

Both times it was an island
in a room with a wide window, a spy hole,
on the sea scrubbing away like an old woman
her wash. A lobsterman hunting for a refund,
gulls like flying babies come by for their dole.
My grandfather typing, He is my little Superman,
he rocks me when the lighthouse flattens her eyes out.
All from the room I pray to when I am dreaming and devout.

August 29, 1971

FEBRUARY 11th

The day is favorable for real-estate affairs.

Houses haunt me.
That last house!
How it sat like a square box!
No closets.
No family room.
Old Oaks bent over city sidewalks.

Still I yearn.
A first home.
A place to take a first baby to.
Railroad tracks
outside the kitchen
window and the good-morning choo-choo.

Tricycles hanging
from the chandeliers.
Kitties like blackboard sharks
nosing their dish.
Buttons and eggs
leaving their little round marks.

A fight
the children called
The Bloody Mary Fight, that worried red

splashed through
the house in the Boston
Strangler way. As if I were dead,

as if I had kissed
the walls in a circle,
hall, kitchen, dining room and back
again. Oh baby bunting,
a first house,
its small mouths, its Union Jack

flying for
our British name.
I'm part Indian I always said
and I was happy there,
part Venetian vase,
part Swiss watch, part Indian head.

August 30, 1971

FEBRUARY 17th

Take nothing for granted.

Yes, I know.
Wallace will be declared king.
For his queen, Shirley Temple Black.
Yes, I know.
The moon will wear garters.
The goldfish will wear a wedding ring.
The chipmunks will subscribe
to the *Old Farmer's Almanac.*
That's just for starters.
Next Queen Elizabeth will take a bribe.
Next the Atlantic will turn to solid ice.
Then the doctors will hand out cancer with their advice.

Yes, I know.
Death sits with his key in my lock.
Not one day is taken for granted.
Even nursery rhymes have put me in hock.
If I die before I wake. Each night in bed.
My husband sings *Baa Baa black sheep* and we pretend
that all's certain and good, that the marriage won't end.

September 1, 1971

69

FEBRUARY 20th

Concentration should be easier.

I concentrate.
My books hypnotize each other.
Jarrell tells Bishop to stare
at the spot. Tate
tells Plath she's going under.
Eliot remembers his long lost mother,
St. Louis and Sweeney who rise out of thin air,
Mr. Boiler Man, his mouth a mountain,
his tongue pure red, his tongue pure thunder,
Hurry up please it's time. Again. Again.

I concentrate.
My typewriter sinks deeper
and deeper. Dear Ruth, Dear John,
Dear Oscar. All dead now. It's late,
hurry up please it's time. Max, surely you're
still here for drinks. Max out, dinner's on.
Max, surely you'll meet me at the Ritz at five.
Hurry up somebody's dead we're still alive.

September 8th, 1971

FEBRUARY 21st

The day is favorable for teamwork.

The photograph where we smile
at each other, dark head to light head,
sits on my desk. It lay unkissed all week.
That photograph walked up the aisle
for the twenty-three years we've been wed
on onward into Carolina, cheek to cheek.
Husband, mad hammer, man of force.
This last week has been our divorce.

I'm not a war baby. I'm a baby
at war. Thumbs grow into my throat.
I wear slaps like a spot of rouge.
Woodsman, who made me into your tree?
Drowner, who made me into your boat?
Lover, I feel a darkness, I feel a fugue
come over us. The photo sits over my desk
as we dance the karate, the mad burlesque.

October 30, 1971

MARCH 4th

Improve your finances.

The high ones, Berryman said, die, die, die.
You look up and who is there?
Daddy's not there shaking his money cane.
Mother's not there waving dollars good-bye
or coughing diamonds into her hanky. Not a forbear,
not an aunt or a chick to call me by name,
not the gardener with his candy dimes and tickles,
not grandpa with his bag full of nickels.

They are all embalmed with their cash
and there is no one here but us kids.
You and me lapping stamps and paying
the bills, shoveling up the beans and the hash.
Our checks are pale. Our wallets are invalids.
Past due, past due, is what our bills are saying
and yet we kiss in every corner, scuffing the dust
and the cat. Love rises like bread as we go bust.

November 22, 1971

MARCH 7th

The day is favorable for creative work.

The big toad sits in my writing room
preventing me from writing. I am a flower
who drys out under her hot breath. She is blowing grass
through her hands! She is knitting up a womb,
knitting up a baby's foot. Her breath is sour.
Her breath is tarnishing up my silver and my brass.
Toad! Are you someone's grunting left-over squaw,
a fat asthmatic Asia, a mother-in-law?

November 22, 1971

73

MAY 30th

Don't look now, God, we're all right.
All the suicides are eating Black Bean Soup;
the Dalmatian, our turnip, our spotted parasite
snoozles in her chair. The trees, that group
of green girls wiggle at every window;
a sea bird, all nude and intimate, comes in low.

The house sinks in its fill, heavy with books;
in the kitchen the big fat sugar sits in a chamber pot;
in the freezer the Blue Fish vomit up their hooks;
the marriage twists, holds firm, a sailor's knot.
Last night he blamed the economy on Roosevelt and Truman.
I countered with Ike and Nixon. Both wrong. Both human.

Please God, we're all right here. Please leave us alone.
Don't send death in his fat red suit and his ho-ho baritone.

May 30, 1971

AUGUST 8th

*And do not be indiscreet or unconventional. Play it
safe.*

Listen here. I've never played it safe
in spite of what the critics say.
Ask my imaginary brother, that waif,
that childhood best friend who comes to play
dress-up and stick-up and jacks and Pick-Up-Sticks,
bike downtown, stick out tongues at the Catholics.

Or form a Piss Club where we all go
in the bushes and peek at each other's sex.
Pop-gunning the street lights like crows.
Not knowing what to do with funny Kotex
so wearing it in our school shoes. Friend, friend,
spooking my lonely hours, you were there, but pretend.

[undated]

AUGUST 17th

Good for visiting hospitals or charitable work. Take
some time to attend to your health.

Surely I will be disquieted
by the hospital, that body zone —
bodies wrapped in elastic bands,
bodies cased in wood or used like telephones,
bodies crucified up onto their crutches,
bodies wearing rubber bags between their legs,
bodies vomiting up their juice like detergent,
bodies smooth and bare as darning eggs.

Here in this house
there are other bodies.
Whenever I see a six-year-old
swimming in our aqua pool
a voice inside me says what can't be told . . .
Ha, someday you'll be old and withered
and tubes will be in your nose
drinking up your dinner.
Someday you'll go backward. You'll close
up like a shoebox and you'll be cursed
as you push into death feet first.

Here in the hospital, I say,
that is not my body, not my body.

I am not here for the doctors
to read like a recipe.
No. I am a daisy girl
blowing in the wind like a piece of sun.
On ward 7 there are daisies, all butter and pearl
but beside a blind man who can only
eat up the petals and count to ten.
The nurses skip rope around him and shiver
as his eyes wiggle like mercury and then
they dance from patient to patient to patient
throwing up little paper medicine cups and playing
catch with vials of dope as they wait for new accidents.
Bodies made of synthetics. Bodies swaddled like dolls
whom I visit and cajole and all they do is hum
like computers doing up our taxes, dollar by dollar.
Each body is in its bunker. The surgeon applies his gum.
Each body is fitted quickly into its ice-cream pack
and then stitched up again for the long voyage
back.

August 17–25, 1971

Three Stories

(1974)

THE GHOST

I was born in Maine, Bath, Maine, Down East, in the United States of America, in the year of 1851. I was one of twelve (though only eight lasted beyond the age of three) and within the confines of that state we lived at various times in our six houses, four of which were scattered on a small island off Boothbay Harbor. They were not called houses on that island for they are summering places and thus entitled cottages. My father, at one time Governor, was actually a frustrated builder and would often say to the carpenters, "another story upwards, please." One house had five stories, and although ugly to look upon, stood almost at the edge of the rocks that the sea locked in and out of.

I was, of course, a Victorian lady, however I among my brothers and sisters was well educated and women were thought, by my father, to be as *interesting* as men, or as capable. My education culminated at Wellesley College, and I was well-versed in languages, both the ancient and unusable as well as the practical, for the years after Wellesley College I spent abroad perfecting the accent and the idiomatic twists. Later I held a job on a newspaper. But it was not entirely fulfilling and made no use of these foreign languages but only of the mother tongue. I was fortunately a maiden lady all my life, and I do say *fortunate* because it allowed me to adopt to maiden heart the nieces and nephews, the grandnieces, the grandnephews. And there was one in particular, my sister's grandchild, who was named after me. And as she wore my name, I wore hers, and at the end of my life she and her mother and an officious practical nurse stood their ground beside me as I went out. Death taking place twice. Once at sixty-four when my ears died and the most ignominious madness overtook me. Next the half-death of sixty shock treatments and then still deaf as a haddock — a half-life until seventy-seven spent in a variety of places called nursing homes. Dying on a hot day in a crib with diapers on. To die like a baby is not desirable and just barely tolerable, for there is fear spooned into you and radios playing in your head. I, the suffragette, I of the violet sachets, I who always changed my dress for dinner and kept my pride, died like a baby with my breasts bared, my corset, my camisole, tucked away, and every other covering that was my custom. I would have preferred the huntsman stalking me like a moose to that drooling away.

There is more to say of my lifetime, but my interest at this point, my main thrust, is to tell you of my life as a ghost. Life? Well, if there is action and a few high kicks, is that not similar to what is called life? At any rate, I *bother* the living, act up a bit, slip like a radio into their brains or a sharp torchlight going on suddenly to blind and then reveal myself. (With no explanation!) I can put a moan into my namesake's dog if I wish to make a point. (I have always liked to make my point!) It is *her* life I linger over, for she is wearing my name and that gives a ghost a certain right that no one knows when they present the newborn with a name. She is somewhat aware — but of course denies it as best she can — that there are any ghosts at all. However, it can be noted that she is unwilling to move into a house that is not newly made, she is unwilling to live within the walls that might whisper and tell stories of other lives. It is her ghost theory.

But like many, she has made the perfect mistake; the mistake being that a ghost belongs to a house, a former room, whereas this ghost (and I can only speak for myself for we ghosts are not allowed to converse about how we go about practicing our trade) belongs to my remaining human, to bother her, to enter the human her, who once was given my name. I could surmise that there are ghosts of houses wading through the attics where once they hoarded their hoard, throwing dishes off shelves, but I am not sure of it. I think the English believe it because their castles were passed on from generation to generation. Indeed, perhaps an American ghost does something quite different, because the people of the present are very mobile, the executives are constantly thrown from city to city, dragging their families with them. But I do not know, for I haunt namesake's, and she lives in the suburbs of Boston — despite a few moves from new house to new house. I follow her as a hunting dog follows the scent, and as long as she breathes, I will peer in her window at noon and watch her sip the vodka, and if I so desire, can place one drop of an ailment into it to teach her a little lesson about such indulgence and imperfection. I gave her five years ago a broken hip. I immobilized her flat on the operating table as I peered over his shoulder, the surgeon said as he did a final x-ray before slicing in with his knife, "shattered," and there was namesake, her hip broken like a crystal goblet and later with two four-inch screws in her hip she lay in a pain that had only been an intimation of pain during the birth of two children. A longing for morphine dominated her hours and her conscience rang in her head like a bell tolling for the dead. She had at the time been committing a major sin, and I found it so abhorrent that it was necessary to make my ailment decisive and sharp. When the morphine was working, she was perfectly lucid, but as it wore off, she sipped a hint of madness and that too was an intimation of things to come. Later, I tried lingering fevers that were quite undiagnosable and then when the world became summer and the green leaves whispered, I sat upon leaf by leaf and called out with a voice of my youth and cried, "Come to us, come to us" until she finally pulled down each shade of the house to keep the leaves out of it — as best she could. Then there are the small things that I can do. I can tear the pillow from under her head at night and leave her as flat as I was when I lay dying and thus crawl into her dream and remind her of my death, lest it be her death. I do not in any way consider myself evil but rather a good presence, trying to remind her of the Yankee heritage, back to the Mayflower and William Brewster, or back to kings and queens of the Continent who married and intermarried. She is becoming altogether too modern, and when a man enters her, I am constantly standing at the bedside to observe and call forth a child to be named my name. I do not actually *watch* the copulation because it is an alien act to me, but I know full well what it should mean and have often plucked out a few of her birth control pills in hopes. But I fear it is a vain hope. She is perhaps too old to conceive, or if she should, the result might be imperfect. As I stand there at that bedside while this man enters her, I hum a little song into her head that we made up, she and I, when she was eight and we sang each year thereafter for years. We had kissed thirteen lucky times over the mistletoe that hung under a large chandelier and two door frames. This mistletoe was *our* custom and *our* act and tied the knot more surely year by year. The song that she sang haunted me in the madness of old age and now I let it enter her ear and at first she feels a strange buzzing as if a fly has been caught in her brain and then the song fills her head and I am at ease.

She senses my presence when she cooks things that are not to my liking, or drives beyond the speed limit, or makes a left turn when it says NO LEFT TURN. For I play in her head the song called "The Stanley Steamer" for Mr. Stanley's wife was my close friend and we took a memorable ride from Boston to Portland and the horses were not happy, but we disobeyed nothing and were cautious — though I must add, a bit dusty and a little worse for wear at the end of the trip.

It is unfortunate that she did not inherit my felicity with the foreign tongue. But not all can be passed on, the genes carry some but not all. As a matter of fact, it is far *more* unfortunate that she did not inherit my gift with the English language. But here I do interfere the most, for I put *my* words onto her page, and when she observes them, she wonders how it came about and calls it "a gift from the muse." Oh how sweet it is! How adorable! How the song of the mistletoe rips through the metal of death and plays on, singing from two mouths, making me a loyal ghost. Loyal though I am I have felt for a long time something missing from her life that she must experience to be whole, to be truly alive. Although one might say it be the work of the devil, I think that it is not (the devil lurks among the living and she must push him out day by day, but first he must enter her as he entered me in my years of deafness and lunacy). Thus I felt it quite proper and fitting to drop such a malady onto a slice of lemon that floated in her tea at 4 P.M. last August. It started immediately and became in the end immoderate. First the teacup became two teacups, then three, then four. Her cigarettes as she lit them in confusion tasted like dung and she stamped them out. Then she turned on the radio and all it would give at every station on the dial were the names and the dates of the dead. She turned it off quickly, but it would not stop playing. The dog chased her tail and then attacked the woodwork, baying at the moon as if their two bodies had gone awry. At that point, she sat very still. She kept telling herself to dial "O" for operator but could not. She shut her eyes, but they kept popping open to see the objects of the kitchen multiply, widen, stretch like rubber and their colors changing and becoming ugly and the lemon floated in the multiplying and dividing teacups like something made of neon.

When her husband returned home, she was as if frozen and could not speak, though I had put many words in her head they were like a game and were mixed and had lost their meaning. He shook her, she wobbled side to side. He spoke, he spoke. For an hour at least he tried for response then dialed the doctor, and she went into Mass. General, half carried, half walking like a drunk, feet numb as erasers, legs melting and stiffening and was given the proper modern physical and neurological exams, EEG, EKG, etc., but the fly in her head still buzzed and the obituaries of the radio played on, and when they took her in an ambulance to a mental hospital, she could not sign her name on the commitment papers but spoke at last, "no name." They could not, those psychiatrists, nurses aides, diagnose exactly and most days she is not able to swallow. The tranquilizers they shot into her, variety after variety, have no power over *this*. I will give her a year of it, an exact to the moment year of it, and during that time, I will be constantly at her side to push the devil from her although there was no one in my time to push him from me. She is at this point enduring a great fear, but I am with her, I am holding her hand and she senses this despite her conviction that each needle is filled with Novocain, for that is the effect on her limbs and parts. Still, the slight pressure of my hand, the sound of the song of the mistletoe must comfort her. Right now they scream to her and fill her with an extraordinary terror. But somehow, I know full well she is indubitably pleased that I have not left. Nor do I plan to.

VAMPIRE

I was a perfectly normal man. As a matter of fact a successful
insurance agent. I could sell death to anyone. I could sell old
age — and its annuities — because my clients felt themselves
stiffen (though they were only twenty-nine or so). I could see
them make up a movie in their head of the "other" — the
other, the aged self — warty, fingers no better than crowbars.
I somehow *put* them there (just for a second) so they would
buy, buy, buy.

Still, two nights ago just off Route 9 on the Jamaica Way,
I struck out. A Doctor, into research, who was just enough of
an ass to think he could cure anything or would invent it at
any moment. No sale. The shit! Oh, well, I thought, you
win some and you lose some, as I scraped off my frozen windshield. Backing out of his unplowed drive, dammit if I didn't
back right over his dog. Unlucky dog — a poodle perhaps, I
thought as I peeked through the glassy windshield, a flattened
poodle lying in the snow like a movie star in too much
ketchup. Didn't stop — serves that Mr. Doctor right, he of
the cure and the research. Right there in his drive I left *my*
answer and drove off thinking, "Not my fault — the dog was
in the way and you, Mr. Doctor, when are you going to be in
someone's way? What cure? What inventions?"

Next day, a new day, a new dollar and the client was a hot
one and thus the buy, buy, buy. He had what it takes — the
terror of no job. For the terror of no job but the body going

on and on, I have the cure — an annuity. For the terror of the body flicking out at any moment, slapped out of you at any age, slapped out like a mosquito, I had the cure — a life insurance policy. Of course I did not insure the life itself, but insured the sudden drop of it and its ability to bring home the bread. I felt like a priest of sorts, insuring them against the luck of it all.

The following day walking down Beacon Street toward the capitol, the sweet gold-domed capitol of Boston, two men (or was it men? I knew right off they were hospital attendants — the white coats to the knee — interns perhaps, or nurses) quickly grabbed me and held both arms to my back in an armlock and shot me with a needle straight through the camel's-hair-Filene's-Basement overcoat, Brooks Brothers jacket, Brooks Brothers shirt, deep into the skin, through the skin of both forearms (oh the skin!) a needle containing a drug — or a potion?

Now let me assure you I was perfectly normal except for a slight fear of escalators swallowing me up — I was normal and brave enough to defy the escalators, therefore better than normal, having overcome the smallest of neuroses. A normal, normal man selling his goods, bringing home the dough for the seven-room house, the wife, the three kids, and I didn't even dream, even there in the queen-size bed. My wife was a wonderful hostess. My children grew step after step from birth to eight and ten. Nothing unexpected. A registered Republican, a Rotary member, a guy among guys who was making it.

That's all I can remember of the old me except for a flowered sugar bowl on the kitchen table that was my grandmother's. A résumé of sorts and a sugar bowl.

Now I am kept in some sort of darkened room. Or perhaps my eyes are glued shut by my keepers, my daytime keepers. I do not see them come or go. I only know that I am unconscious all day — if there still *is* a day with a sun in it or a blue sky and all that from my other life. At any rate, what I call "day" is my time of sleep, a drugged sleep but one cannot be sure of such things. I can only note that I do not dream here either.

When I wake twelve bells ring, and I find with my blind fingers a costume folded at the end of my bed — it is a rubber skin diver's suit and fits me exactly. On top of it is an address book. I did not at first know what kind of book but saw in the streetlights when I went forth. There is also a rather surprising loaf of French bread, and I realize that I must put on the rubber suit, the sneakers. And the bread — it is surely the most surprising of all, for the aroma floats upward, freshly baked, still warm to the touch. I am hungry, terribly hungry and yet I realize it is to go with the meal that I must seek. An invisible order that seems to have been written out in my head, and so on with the suit, sneakers, carrying in my left hand the address book and under my right arm the bread I walk forth onto the streets of Boston.

Under a streetlight I inspected for the first time the book, the address book which was entitled "Girls" and there were separate sections, headings such as *Playboy Club* or *Topless Dancers*, etc. No names were included but addresses, apartment numbers, directions and all that was necessary for the job.

Out into the night I went and have done so compulsively from then on, up and down Beacon Hill or Back Bay or even into the suburbs (if I have a feel for it) to find the half-open ground floor window waiting and softly raise it and enter. I have but one purpose.

Zip off the covers — ah, there she is, *this one,* lovely and waiting. Oh the sirloin steak of her! The juice waiting inside the dull-pink flesh (each one, night by night, year by year, I call "this one!").

And as is my custom (I try not to call it a compulsion because I think it would unnerve me in my mission — it is best not to give names to too many things or to dig into the mystery and its rituals) I put my mouth to her belly button — that which held her to her mother to her mother to her mother — back into the eternal . . . I dig my teeth in that belly until I can suck, suck out the red juice. The blood, the darling of her blood, filling my mouth, oh the filling of my mouth — hold it there! Hold it inside the mouth for a minute or two, rinsing it back and forth between my teeth, letting my tongue swim in it like a fish and letting all the taste enter the senses, like tasting the ocean, salty, salty, causing the addiction, falling in love with the addiction and then swallowing. To feed! To feed! There is such love in it — a transfusion body to body. This is repeated three magical times and then a short break for the bread — somewhat like her tummy — also the tough crust that is like the knot of her belly button.

And what of her? Do I only dream that she cries out in joy? There is a cry, but it might be silent, just a gape of the mouth, with a ghost floating out. Have I hurt you? I ask, each time that I rest to munch the bread, but I never get an answer. She is very still, but that is proper. Are you okay? I asked the first time, and when that first one only opened her mouth and no sound issued toward me, my own voice spoke up in my head. Food! Food! It is perfectly proper and absolutely necessary to have food. Think of the starving Armenians, said the grandmothers of yesteryear. I starve. I eat. Plain common sense. Blood and bread, blood and bread, but human blood only, woman blood only. It must be thus. It was ordained.

At first I rationalized, thinking of transplants, and IVs and plasma and the transfusions that save the helpless. I have become a one-man hospital, I am helpless to stop this, this saving my life, myself and with no Blue Cross, no taking up a hospital bed and bothering nurses. Just this little crawl into a girl's room, to borrow, to suck, until I am full for a night. One does what one must and although it's an unusual encounter — navel and mouth — the blood filling me in an hour or two, as my heart does well, pumping it toward toes, fingers, brain and all necessary parts. I do not know if I use up all her blood — perhaps it is so — but I prefer not to dwell on the results of that. I prefer to think of her blood as a gift, a miraculous gift. When it is over, I tuck her in snugly, smoothing the covers, and as I go out the window, I shut it tightly but softly, lest she feel a bit of a chill.

THE BAT
or
TO REMEMBER, TO REMEMBER

There I was at the judgment court, badly needing a shave, having sat outside for days and days, the case load is too much, poorly handled I'd say, and the dead sit in rows on stone benches, waiting and waiting until their number is called. Perhaps this is part of the plan — to wait and wait — gnawing at your tongue, watching the door open and someone make his exit. We stare into the eyes or at the mouths or sometimes the hands of those who exit. It is hard to know what their verdicts have been for each shows anxiety of a different sort and though we sometimes ask, run up and beat at their chests, "What happened? What's your verdict?" they only do one thing — put their thumbs against their mouths to keep them shut. The anxiety builds. No one weeps, but otherwise there are moans, soft, soft moans like a chorus turned down low lest it be overheard.

Then someone's number is called and they rise and rush for the door as if they were on fire and running from it. When, after three weeks and twenty-nine hours, I was called — my number, I realized, was my Social Security number. "Good God," I shouted, "the same God-damned number even HERE!"

Moans. Moans. Louder in spite of themselves. Then I rushed forward even faster than others had, because I had made that mistake of telling something. Perhaps I had only *thought* it — not *shouted* it — but the point was I *knew* it and no one else had ever spoken out that fact, and perhaps they did not know it was their number from life. After all, we had sat there and had remembered nothing — not a single event, picture, the speech of our lives — not *any* of it. And there I was — in a flash — remembering my Social Security number and when I should have held it dear I swore at it instead. And in such a place! Where anything could happen!

"Perhaps my whole life will be put on like a movie in the courtroom?" I thought, and that is why I was given this intimation. There must be facts stated: the truth, I swear to tell, I swear to hear, I will not perjure, etc., etc.

Not so, I was to find. I entered and it was absolutely dark, blacker than blindness. A voice spoke to me, or rather to my number. It was a tiny voice as if it would rather squeak than make words with its voice box. Then a small, pinpoint light flashed on the voice and there, on a small stool sat a marionette, or as far as I could comprehend, it was a marionette. Strings moved its hands and feet, and it was, I do believe, made of wood. It was dressed in a plush sort of suit that had no more color than the tiny light had a color. But what it said to me was, "Stand back Number 032-24-9806, for I have your judgment."

"Have I no lawyer, no defender, no rights in the matter?" I asked as ingratiatingly as I could.

"Your life is your defense, and I have observed it all along," it beeped out.

"And witnesses?" I asked, meeker, more fearful.

"The people in your life," it said.

Then I felt numb, wondering what it had been, this life I had led, and who were my people, and had I been worthy of a good judgment perhaps or a bad one or — ? And then I thought of the others, on the other side of the door, and I spoke out for them, perhaps selfishly, trying to show that I was thoughtful, compassionate, even *here*, even *here*, to show plainly that I felt for ALL MAN — not just for me. And I spoke out for them and asked if all judgments were the same, and if all were dealt with fairly and justly in this last courtroom. A string pulled, and it stamped its tiny foot. "Nothing of them will you ever know, and, as you exit, if you speak, your verdict will immediately reverse itself, and that always goes badly, quite badly. Thumb to your mouth, if they ask, if they plead, if they try to pound it out of you — just this, thumb to your mouth to lock it up."

"Justice . . . Justice . . ." I mumbled, but it did not seem to hear.

"Nothing will they know, except what they see, which is unavoidable because we are cramped for space though it has its assets for those who wait are not alone."

"Not exactly," I replied with a touch of sarcasm knowing how alone it is out there, waiting, waiting — but for what?

And here it was. The judgment court and a marionette running the whole show. I blurted it out. I could not help it. "Who pulls your strings? Who speaks through your mouth?"

"Me! Me!" it said, stamping both its tiny feet and opening its arms wide and then clapping the stick fingers.

"My verdict? Quick, quick, my verdict!" I screamed knowing my defenses were falling off me, and I could stand the tension no longer.

"Dear 032-24-9806," he said. "You are to be rewarded for the ninth time in this courtroom with REINCARNATION. You will be warm-blooded — but not of the same species."

"Will I have the nine lives to remember, the fruit of them, the wisdom that accumulates too late?"

"Somewhat."

"I have to remember, I must, I must — "

"More than you might wish."

"But alive. Alive!" I swelled with the thought, the deep inner need to live.

"Somewhat."

"May I — "

"You *may* exit now, thumb-locking the mouth and live upon the earth for your tenth time."

I was removed — out numbly through the room of moans, and they beat hard on me, and I kept locked lest the decision be reversed.

Here I am — a bat. Bat? Life? To dine on insects, to catch them with my radar, to be next door to blind, to hang upside down all day, to go down chimneys by mistake. Is that life? But all incidental to the remembering, the terrible mixture of nine human lives relived each day as I hang upside-down and the lives themselves seem to hang upside down — and it is not good, this mixture, the mad photograph album, the voices, all nine, saying something wise from one life and being cut into at the vital moment — with a Cut for the ADVERTISEMENT! —

and then with Jane (me) saying, "I ripped up the drapes, Mother, so everyone could see in and watch what *you* do to me."

Cut!

— ADVERTISEMENT —

and then "Son," says George (me), "do not leave college. I had the hands of a surgeon but I got her with child and then what I did, I can't face what I did. I tell you — "

Cut!

— AD —

and then

Movie set — cameras rolling on another life. Two in bed, touching, licking, biting and then she says, "Jeffy, put it in," and as I start to —

Cut!

— AD —

and then Me, baby Janet, spitting out the breast and the milk spurting onto the wallpaper and my bawling and bawling (and I want to hold me, to make it better, to put the breast back, I want to change that baby, that Janet me) and magic! it happens and the breast pops in again but now there is no milk left and the mother says —

Cut!

— AD —

and then on and on, part by mixed up part, the characters getting into the wrong lives, crawling into different decades or centuries — but there is one life constantly cutting in, the life that only shows one drama that repeats and repeats: THE AD — but this, this vignette of the last life — doesn't punch out so quickly.

And yet it is the AD — a complete scenario — A man (me) living in a rooming house on Marlborough Street and soup on the hot plate and stew on the hot plate. The room with a high ceiling, a crystal chandelier, but the paint peeling in strips and the roaches, when you snap on the light, washing away in different black directions. The sound of cars, college kids or street kids selling *The Phoenix* or *Boston After Dark*.

Then a girl's scream, one night around ten, and a girl running on her high heels down the icy sidewalk, and a man calling out, "GET THE POLICE."

I run out and karate the man at the back of the neck. He slumps. "Good, you bastard, she doesn't need a cop. Or at least she doesn't need YOU."

She pulls me to her and sobs on my sweaty shirt. Sobs and sobs. I know I have saved her, but from what? I ask and ask and she just keeps crying and then I ask her name, and she says, "I've forgotten."

And then I ask her if I can take her home, and she says, "Yes. Home, I want to go home. I am afraid."

"Okay, Miss No-name, which way is home? I'll take you there," trying to cheer her up.

"I've forgotten where it is — I can't remember the address."

What's a guy to do with talk like that? So I take her to my room and she quickly kneels by my bed and whispers to it, over and over. "Can you let me in on it?" I ask wondering what the fuck is this? After some hours of me sitting beside her as she kneels and whispers, I begin to feel dizzy and queer. I begin to listen to something, is it her whispering prayer? I feel more and more like a creep and begin to wonder if it's a dream (after all, I am upside down, only a bat, can this be part of a *real* life?) But in this life the living are getting upside down, too. The man whom I karated calls from the street below into a bullhorn I guess, the sound being like one.

He shouts, "TAKE THE NAILS OUT OF THE TOP DRAWER FOR THE SHELVES YOU WERE GOING TO PUT UP. TAKE THE HAMMER OUT OF THE TOP DRAWER FOR THE SHELVES YOU WERE GOING TO PUT UP."

And I do, and I do. Then I stand holding nails and hammer and wait as if there were a reasonable reason. The girl rises, as he calls up to her to do so and then it's Him, Him,

Him *telling, commanding,* and we are the actors in His play. (Bat-me thinks, "He's a director and she's an actress and maybe I'm in a movie by mistake?")

From the bullhorn, "MISS NO-NAME, GO INTO THE CLOSET AND FLATTEN AGAINST THE WALL."

She does. She goes into the closet and flattens against the wall.

"SPREAD OUT YOUR ARMS LIKE A SCARE-CROW."

She does. She spreads out her arms like a scarecrow.

"TWIST YOUR ANKLES AROUND EACH OTHER."

She does. She twists her ankles around each other.

("I'm only a bat," I say to myself. "I just don't get this movie, this AD. What are they advertising? What are they selling?")

It keeps right on going on. "TAKE ONE NAIL AND HAMMER IT INTO HER PALM," he shouts.

I do. I see it, I see the blood spurt, I see the nail sink through flesh and into the wood. She does not move.

"TAKE ANOTHER NAIL AND HAMMER IT INTO HER OTHER PALM."

The same. And under command, at each move, I drive the longest nails through her ankles. She does not even flinch.

"DRIVE YOUR HUNTING KNIFE THROUGH HER CHEST."

I am suddenly wild. I open and shut drawers. I open and shut the two windows. I pull the bed over on top of me and still he calls for the hunting knife.

"IT'S IN THE MEDICINE CABINET."

I go to the cabinet. The knife is sitting there. Thrust! Thrust! Sideways to slip between the ribs. She cries out in a foreign language and dies for twenty hours as I stand watching — watching, hearing nothing but her gasps, slower and slower until they are gone. Then with no bullhorn, no voice from the director from the sidewalk, I nail the door shut and walk out.

Cut!

All the time this scene is relived I, a simple bat, am shaking and gasping. I am in a state of horror. Next I beat myself against the trunks of trees, buildings, walls, anything hard that my radar senses.

It doesn't shut it out.

She was Miss No-name, and I was only a man, not remembering what to call myself when I relived myself in that life — the AD. What was it selling? What kind of life held a scene like that? I sense that was my last reincarnation, I mean the ninth, the last one where I was of the species called human.

So many moments, mixed into each other from different lives, at different ages and the wrong wives talking to the wrong husbands or the sister talking to the baby I aborted (perhaps an eighth life) and the Great Aunt pouring tea from a Spode pitcher and asking (a fourth life perhaps) though she always knew, "Lemon, dear, or milk?"

Cut!

— AD —

"Spit out the breast, baby Janet."

Cut!

— AD —

"Put it into me, put it into me," and I start to and . . .

Cut!

THE AD, total in its twenty-four hours — always interrupting and never saying why or who or how come.

As daylight descends and I go to my place, I say one thing over and over, "I WILL REMEMBER NOTHING. I WILL REMEMBER NOTHING. I am only a bat. I was born a bat. I will die a bat. I WILL REMEMBER NOTH-ING. I WILL REMEMBER NOTHING." But I do. I am locked into it.

I wish I could peer into your window at night, and speak in the human voice I had nine times and say something to your snuggling pillowy head of this, this damnation. But you would wake and scream, then with a shaking hand take a pill and at last go back to sleep again, not knowing that the night-mare at your window is living, and reliving, his upside-down lives and maybe, poor sleeper, even one of yours.